BREAKFAST AT KATSOURIS

by

Bill Rogers

First Paperback Edition

Published in May 2014 by Caton Books

Whilst this book is based on factual research, and actual police operations are referred to as background context, all of the characters in this book are fictitious, and any resemblance, if any, to actual persons, living or dead, is purely coincidental. Any references to businesses, organisations, places or localities are intended only to give the fiction a sense of authenticity. With the sole exception of Katsouris. DCI Caton's favourite Deli.

All of the events and behaviours described as taking place in those settings were fictional.

Published by Caton Books as a *Caton's Quickies* imprint

Paperback ISBN: 978-1-909856-09-7

Cover Design by Dragonfruit
Design & Layout: Commercial Campaigns

www.catonbooks.com
www.billrogers.co.uk

Contents

Breakfast at Katsouris

He fled like a startled deer, his heart pounding in his chest. His breath came in gulps, and fire burned in the muscles of his legs. Pumping his arms, he veered past the climbing frame, hoping against hope; knowing that he wasn't going to make it. Twin shards of pain punched through his thighs a millisecond before his brain registered the sound of gunfire. Floundering like a fish, his scream slicing through the air, he pitched forward. There was cold steel against the back of his head...

The bulldozers rolled in ten years before Caton was born. Homely Victorian terraced streets replaced by the Crescents; grey, high rise, deck-access concrete blocks. The close community of extended families, including his own, scattered to the winds. By the time he was twenty these cities in the sky were slums where the old, infirm, and vulnerable hid behind plywood doors and grey net curtains. A no-go area for all but the brave and foolhardy. Then the regeneration plan took root. South Central Manchester had been transformed.

Where dealers dealt and scores were settled, where prostitutes and rent boys once plied their trade, two acres of green field park now spread out before him.

Surrounded by angled railings above a metre high brick wall, there are no hiding places. There is a podium, a canopied performance area, a basketball court, and a cluster of picnic tables. Speed bumps and stainless steel bollards keep out the stolen cars and motor bikes. Sixties slums have been replaced by superior flats, and brand new houses to appeal to young professionals working in the city centre less than a mile away. Crime has plummeted. Gentrification was the term the media used. Economic eviction was what Caton's father had called it, before the accident that took him and his wife, and spared their son.

At seven o'clock on this late October evening, cleared by the cordon of officers lining the perimeter, the park is cold, damp, and gloomy. Over by the Treasure Island playground, with its dunes and shipwrecks, the trees have lost their canopy of golden leaves now drifting over impact cushioning surfaces. The unmistakeable smell of hops drifts across from the Royal Brewery on Princess Parkway. He shivers as a light drizzle sweeping in from the Irish Sea sends icy tendrils down the back of his neck. It isn't true that it always rains in Manchester, it only feels like it. Forlorn pools of light heighten his sense of alienation as he pulls up the hood of his Tyvek barrier suit and sets off towards the shadowy huddle at the southern end of the playground.

'One down Boss,' said DS Holmes, plucking at his chin with a latex glove. 'We've got a name for him. Marvin Brown, drug supplier and amateur gunsmith. This gives us probable motive.'

'Does that mean that we know who the perpetrators are Gordon?'

He shrugged his shoulders like a prop forward preparing for a scrum.

'DI Tyldesley says she has some names.'

Detective Inspector Tyldesley, fast track female

deputy chief of the Xcalibre Task Force; the Greater Manchester Police initiative that had broken the stranglehold of gun crime in the city. As bright as she was bonny. Rumours abounded as to the reasons for her single status. Caton only cared that she was good at what she did.

'Duty pathologist is on her way,' Holmes told him. 'Not that there's any doubt about the cause of death.'

Caton followed him towards the circle of harsh white light from twin flood lamps.

The victim lay face up, sprawled across the children's roundabout. A mixed-race male in his late forties. His head, torso, and legs, squeezed between the central struts, arms flung wide between the gaps on either side. Blood had spread from an ugly hole at the front of his neck, fanlike, across his leather jacket. Identical holes had been torn through both thighs above the knee. Bled out, his face had a copper sheen that matched the too familiar smell of blood, like rusting iron.

'Those are exit wounds?' said Caton. Their shape, and the way the jagged edges of the cloth splayed outwards, left little room for doubt.

'Yes Sir,' replied the crime scene manager. 'It looks like he was shot from behind, over there.' She pointed back up the path towards a climbing frame and the granite slab that locals nicknamed Zion Square. 'Then he was shot through the base of his neck, close up, execution style.'

Caton could see a dark patch where blood had pooled, and parallel tracks that smeared the path.

'His body was dragged over here, and displayed like this?'

She nodded. 'They must have spun the roundabout.'

He could see the crimson star burst sprayed in a circle across the blue composition surface.

'It spirals ever closer,' she said. 'Where the roundabout slowed down, and his heart stopped pumping.'

The action played in his mind like a video nasty.

'Any witnesses?'

'A woman walking her dog by the Zion Centre, two youths on the BMX jump track, and another five having a kick around on the football pitch,' Holmes told him. 'Plus anyone in the flats who might have been out on their balconies. We won't know till we get the results of the door to door.'

'Presumably the ones we do know about would have heard the initial shots, and seen the gunman?'

'Gun*men*,' said Holmes. 'Two of them on mountain bikes. They went off towards Castlefield, but I doubt if anyone will ID them. Hoods up…the light was failing…didn't get a clear view…all happened so fast. You know how it is Boss. Self preservation.'

It explained why they'd taken their time. Dumping the body like that. Spinning it round. Sticking up two fingers to the police, and to their own community. *This is our turf. We do what we want. And there's not a damn thing you can do about it.*

'We haven't had a shooting, Tom, since last July.' Jean Tyldesley tucked a wayward strand of auburn hair inside her hood. 'The good news is the list of likely suspects has shrunk since we put the last lot inside.'

'They must be covered in blood, not to mention the residue from the gun.'

'My team are onto it,' she told him. 'We know their home addresses, and bolt holes, and most of their associates. I'll have them sent over to your incident room.'

Caton took the ramp onto the Mancunian Way. Seventy two hours. The equivalent for a murder inquiry of the paramedic's golden hour. After that it was as good as a cold case. The rain had ceased. His headlights picked out the towering glass and steel of the University buildings, dwarfed by the floodlit shard of the Beetham Tower. In the gaps between the redbrick warehouse apartments by the canal he caught glimpses of late night revellers making their way towards the Gay Village, Chinatown, and the bustling bars and pavement cafes in the centre of this twenty four hour city. It was going to be a late night for everyone. It would be a miracle if he managed breakfast.

He hugged his seventh mug of coffee and stared at the head shots on the white board. Four black, seven white, three Asian. All males. Shaven heads, hard eyes, defiant stares. Lost souls, not one of them over twenty one.

'I'm sorry,' said Tyldesley. 'But of the three hundred gang members known to us those are the most likely; but like I said it's been quiet out there for months.'

'The ones on the right have alibis,' he told her. 'The rest have all tested negative for firearm discharge residue. There's not a spot of blood on any of them.'

'That's a miracle in itself,' she muttered.

He checked the clock on the wall of the Incident Room. Ten hours gone. Brown's wallet, full of cash, was still in his jacket. His flat had been alarmed and untouched when they'd searched it. They had nothing from the cameras. That was the trouble with mountain bikes, they rat-ran down the ginnels and back alleys. No word from the streets either. Tyldesley was right; there wasn't a hint of gang involvement.

He went over to the list headed *Motive?* One by one he struck them through with the dry marker. *Gang Vengeance; Robbery; Thrill; Initiation; Mental Illness; Crime of Passion; Hate Crime; Contract Killing.* His marker hovered over the remaining three: *Disrespect; Jealousy; Revenge.* He walked to the window to clear his mind.

The sunlight crept like a thief from behind the Pennine Hills, pushing aside the inky blackness of Saddleworth Moor, painting crimson the belly of clouds the colour of cobalt. Slowly it spread across Eastlands, caressing the smooth concrete curves of the Commonwealth Stadium and the Velodrome, dancing lightly across the water in the Piccadilly basin, before reaching up to flame the windows in front of him. Red sky in the morning, shepherd's warning.

He turned to face them.

'Gordon, have you got that log of observations the Drugs Team had been doing on Brown's flat?'

Holmes returned with the file. Along with the notes there were photographs of people coming and going. He spread them out on the desk top.

This one,' said Caton.

A young woman leaving at five in the morning. She wore a thin white blouse over a short, tight, pencil skirt - little more than a pelmet - with a pair of six inch high-heeled shoes.

'Who is she?'

Diane Tyldesley leant over him, her hair brushing his cheek. A tiny jolt of static passed between them. She didn't seem to notice. He caught a whiff of perfume, Jo Malone, Pomegranate Noir. It had been his wife's favourite.

'I think its Danny Wilkes's girl friend,' she said straightening up. 'He's a minnow with the

Wythenshawe Rottweiler Crew.'

She arrived at midnight, and left at five in the morning.' Caton said pointedly.

'Looks like he might have started swimming in a big pool,' said Gordon Holmes as he reached for the phone.

They watched her through the observation window. She was terrified and distraught. Not by the questions they had asked, by the enormity of what she'd triggered.

'That's it then,' said Holmes, a trifle too gleefully for Caton's liking. 'Danny Wilkes, strutting his stuff, took his woman to a meet with Brown. I say woman, look at her, all of seventeen. Legs up to her arm pits, skirt shorter than a pelmet, belly button ring, tight tee shirt, no bra. Marvin took a fancy to her, and she sussed out straight away who was the bigger man of the two. Danny with a mountain bike, Marvin with a Mercedes. Not rocket science is it? Marvin gets inside her pants, Danny finds out.' He made a gun with two fingers, and the thumb of his right hand. 'Boom Boom! Good night Marvin Brown.'

Caton watched as she screwed up her tee shirt like a handkerchief, and started to sob into it. Shannon Travis, sixteen years of age. She was young enough to have been his daughter...if they'd got round to children.

'It had to have been something personal,' he said. 'Close up like that. Splayed on the roundabout. He was sending a message. Nobody makes a fool of Danny Wilkes and walks away.'

'But she wasn't there,' said Holmes. 'All she knows for certain is that he'd found out about her and Brown, and he went ballistic.'

Caton nodded. 'So now all we have to do is prove it.'

They took the motorway, sirens blaring to part the rush hour traffic that threatened daily to turn this artery into a car park. As they crested Barton Bridge the rest of Caton's world spread out before him. To his left, the iconic toast rack, home to Manchester United, a cluster of cranes where Media City rose like a phoenix from the ashes, and the baroque temple to retail heaven they'd named the Barton Centre. The Cheshire Plain, with its stockbroker belt and footballer's mansions, spread south and west. On the distant horizon the Snowdonia mountain range was capped with snow. Up ahead a plane took off from the airport at Wythenshawe, and turned lazily north, towards the Lake District.

Wythenshawe, once the largest council estate in Europe. Home to TV cult show *Shameless*. Home to Danny Wilkes. They switched off their sirens but there was no need. A patrol car and a van were already parked.

'We were called to a domestic in there,' the young constable explained, pointing to the former council house behind him.

You could tell by the neat garden, the PVC windows, and the sky blue paintwork. Next door had rotting window frames, a Ford Escort rusting on the concrete lawn, and an ancient German shepherd that hadn't the energy to bark at them.

'Two lads having a right go at each other, and the mother of one of them trying to break it up. As soon as they saw us the lads legged it. We gave chase. Cornered them in a vacant industrial unit over there.' He pointed vaguely towards Benchill.

'Where are they now?' said Caton.

'In the van. We found nothing on them, so we're about to let them go.'

'Over my dead body.' Holmes growled as he strode towards the van.

'The gun is still missing,' said Caton. 'Tactical Aid found a pair of bloodstained trainers, and a load of half burnt clothes at the bottom of a bin round the back of the industrial unit where they tried to hide. If they hadn't run we might never have found them.' He smiled. 'You know what they say...if the clothes fit.'

'And they did?' said Diane Tyldesley.

'The trainer's were Danny's, all of the clothes belonged to one or the other. The blood is Marvin Brown's. Danny's pal was quick to confess. Danny planned it, Danny did the shooting, Danny made him help move the body. He had no idea any of it was going to happen.'

'Naturally.'

'Which should be worth a minimum of seven years, and upwards of twelve, for him.'

'And life for Danny,' she said.

No consolation for Marvin Brown, he reflected, but then he had probably supplied the gun that killed him. Caton had watched with satisfaction and relief the rapid decline in gun crime in Manchester. Now he feared that frontline cuts, and the rising tide in youth unemployment, would see a return to the bad old *Gun*chester days.

'It's the totally senseless waste of young lives that gets to me,' he said.

'Me too,' she agreed. 'But we're doing the best we can.'

He checked his watch, and nodded wearily.

'Fifty six hours to spare,' he said. 'That's almost a record.' He picked up his jacket, and shrugged it on. 'I don't know about you but I'm starving.'

She smiled. 'I think the paperwork can wait.'

'Right then,' he said, opening the door and waving her through.

'Breakfast at Katsouris?'

The Wren Boy

The Writer's Bar of the Listowel Arms Hotel was heaving. On the polished mahogany counter patient rows of rich black Guinness waited for the creamy clouds swirling through them to settle. Whisky chasers passed from hand to hand. In the window bay a fiddle player, a guitarist, a flautist, and a young man playing the traditional bodhran drum, were in full flow. As far as Niamh could tell, every seat was taken.

'You'll never get a drink in a month of Sundays,' a young man standing beside her confided. 'Will you hang on a minute?' He reached over the shoulders of the man in front of him, and poked in the back the one being served. 'Make it another one Michael...a double!' He shouted. Then he turned to face her. 'What's your name if you don't mind me asking?'

'It's Niamh.'

'Well I'm Sean,' he said grinning. 'So now we've been properly introduced, you better come and sit with us. It's either that, or stand up all night.'

He led her through the crush to a group of seats his companions were guarding beside a fire blazing in the ancient black iron fireplace.

After Sean had introduced the others he asked her. 'So what are you doing here in Listowel then?'

She told him how her parents had died in a boating tragedy several years before, and her Aunt Miriam – the last of the family - had been killed less than a month ago in a hit and skip accident in her home town, Manchester, in New Hampshire, USA. How she had decided to trace her family tree, and was over here trying to find distant cousins she believed to be living in North Kilfeighny.

'I am truly sorry for your loss,' he said. 'Let's hope it takes a turn for the better now you're in Ireland.'

Amen to that, thought Niamh. She knew that this obsession with her roots was a desperate attempt to come to terms with the fact that she had never had the chance to say goodbye to her parents and her aunt; to tell them how much she had loved them, and still did. To find some sort of closure. To be able to cry.

Soothed by the warmth of the fire, and the whisky coursing through her veins, she settled back to listen to the music of the Wren Boys' Bands.

Several sets later the MC for the evening stood up.

'And now,' he said. 'Noel Carmody will share with us his remembrance of St Stephen's Day 1913.'

An old man, a lifetime etched on his face, was helped to a seat in front of the band. They brought him a large glass of whisky, and a tumbler of water. He took a sip of each, and began. His voice was rich and strong, not reedy and tremulous as she had expected.

'We heard them coming,' he began. 'From way over the other side of the hill. The flute, the tin whistle, and the throbbing sound of the bodhran as they beat their way to our door. With us being the furthest from the village, it was late when they came. We children had been waiting all day, and were excited and frightened at the very same time. As was our mother, a God fearing woman who thought all of this a terrible heathen practice, which of course it was, but who was caught up in the tradition like the rest of us.'

He cleared his throat, and took a sip of whisky.

"Will they really have caught and killed a wren, Dada?" My little sister Caitlin asked.

"Sure I doubt it," my father replied. "There was a time when they did, but even then they would have kept it alive, and carried it around in a wicker cage for all to see."

She wasn't for letting him off that easy.

"And then would they have set it free Dada?"

My father caught our mother's eye. He patted our Caitlin on the head. "Sure they would," he said, though none of us boys believed him. We knew that the whole point was to sacrifice the wren, to drive out the winter, bring back the sun, and hasten the spring. "That," he had once confided to us boys. "And to get as much money out of the terrified old biddies as possible."

He took another sip, letting the tension mount.

'By now the noise was upon us, and the dogs were howling in the yard.

"You'd best call the dogs off before they beat them with their cudgels." Our mother told him. Father upped and opened the door, yelling at the dogs until one after the other they slunk inside, and took their favourite positions either side of the fire. I plucked up my courage, and went and stood beside my father.'

He paused, and stared right through us.

'They appeared, like ghosts, through a curtain of snow that fell in silent feathery flakes. There were seven of them. Their hats and coats were made of oat straw. What little could be seen of their faces was painted white. The noise they made was deafening. Those not playing the instruments held shillelagh in their hands to beat off the dogs and discourage the competition. Their leader held a pole aloft, from the end of which dangled a wretched wren. Dead as a door nail. My father blocked the doorway.

"If you want to come in, you'll set that down out here," he commanded. "You'll not frighten my children."

I was worried that some of them would remember this, and that I would have to face their taunts in the village. As it happened, they were more frightened of my brothers than they were eager to enjoy my discomfort. One by one they trooped into the house until the room was full. We stood at the margins, and watched as they danced, and whirled, and sang their songs. One of them grabbed my arm, dragged me into the midst of them, twirling until my head was dizzy and my feet left the floor. Our mother brought each of them a buttermilk scone, a thimble of hedgerow wine mulled in the pot over the fire, and a farthing.'

He smiled to himself, and shook his head gently from side to side.

'She said it was for the entertainment they'd given us, but we knew it was for luck. For all her great faith, the old superstitions held sway at times like this.'

He smiled, and looked around the room.

'Sure, it's a rare man can say he's never bet each way at the races.'

He poured a little water into his tumbler of whisky, took a sip, and continued.

'The snow had picked up by now, and there was a wind that threatened to pile it in drifts where a donkey could fall in a ditch, and never get out again. They made their goodbyes, and trooped out into the yard. Their leader took up his pole, and headed for the gate with the rest behind him. The flute kicked off, and then the whistles, and then the boy with the bodhran beat the hell out of the goatskin, and set the jingles jangling, till those of us inside were dancing again. I stood at the door, with the dogs at my heels, and watched as they as disappeared, wraithlike, into the night.'

This time he paused for a good half a minute, staring out beyond the audience as though he could see them still. The room was hushed; nobody moved.

He took up the tumbler of water, drank a little, and placed it carefully back down on the table. He wiped his lips with a handkerchief he was clutching in his left hand, and then continued.

'Of the boys that came that night six of them joined the Royal Munster Fusiliers...and perished together on the battlefields of Europe. Barry Monaghan, the one that led them to our door, charged a machine gun emplacement that had pinned down his platoon, and died a hero. One made a life for himself over the water. One became a priest...and the other a farmer like his father before him.'

With some difficulty, he stretched himself to his full height.

'So I'd like you to join me in a toast.' He raised his tumbler of whisky. 'To the Wren Boys. May the Lord keep them in his hand, and never close his fist too tight!'

Niamh stood with the others. The sweet, smooth, amber spirit sent a warm glow through her body. The old man was not quite finished. He had saved a measure in the bottom of his glass.

'And I've a toast from me, to you,' he said. 'May you never resent growing old, for there's many denied the privilege?'

He drained his glass to a standing ovation, and slammed it down on the table top. A glass with a double measure appeared as if by magic, and was placed in front of him. The band struck up, the crowd began to clap and sing.

'The Wran, the wran, the king of all Birds,
On St. Stephen's Day, it was caught in the furze,
Although he was little, his honour was great,
So jump up me lads, and give him a trate,
Up with the kettle, and down with the pan,
Give us a penny, to bury the wran.'

Niamh discovered her feet had a mind of their own, tapping out the tune like she'd known it forever. It was close to midnight when she made her way to her room. She checked for emails on the laptop, read a few pages of her book, then switched out the light, and drifted off to sleep; lulled by muffled sounds from the bar of the fiddle, the flute and the bodhran.

It was pitch black when Niamh awoke. Despite the duvet she felt as cold as ice. She remembered the spare blanket in the wardrobe, switched on the bedside lamp... and froze in terror, the scream trapped in her throat. A man stood at the foot of the bed. He wore a uniform of rough brown woollen cloth, a thick leather belt around his jacket, and on his head a cap with a golden badge. His face was half in shadow. She sensed that he was smiling.

She clutched the duvet tightly, hands crossed at the neck in the vain hope that it would provide protection. And yet...it was not a malevolent smile. A sad smile perhaps; like the one she'd become accustomed to seeing every morning, in the mirror.

'What do you want?' She whispered.

He turned his face towards the light. A young man with bright blue eyes. The smile now reassuring. He nodded once. Then slowly faded, like breath on a windowpane.

On the desk his body had masked, her lap top glowed in the darkness. Still clutching the duvet, she lowered her feet tentatively to floor, crossed to the desk, and sat down in front of the screen. It was open at the Home page of The Royal Munster Fusiliers. On the left of the banner was a regimental crest, on the right a brass cap badge with a golden flame and a sliver tiger passant. She searched the archives until at last she discovered a sepia photograph of her mysterious visitor. The same face, the same smile; beneath it the legend:

"Barry Monaghan. Hero of Etreux."

She recalled the old man's words.

"Barry Monaghan, the one that led them to our door, charged a machine gun emplacement that had pinned down his platoon, and died a hero."

Returning to the Home page, Niamh read again the words written across the banner.

"To live in the hearts of those we leave behind, is not to die."

Softly, she began to cry.

The Readers

I turned the envelope over and examined the strong, confident handwriting, backward sloping, with long loops and pronounced curlicues. I looked it up one day when I was dabbling with handwriting analysis. Apparently it had all the hallmarks of someone with strong emotions held in check. A person who might appear, on the outside, to be indifferent to others.

It had always surprised me that my grandmother was able to create such complex and sensitive characters in her novels. That implied a capacity for empathy that was never apparent in her dealings with others. Except, that is, for me.

I slid the paper knife under the seal, eased it open, and took out the sheets within. I set the knife down, settled back, and began to read.

Dearest Alice,

You will, no doubt, be wondering why I have left the bulk of my considerable estate to you.

Firstly, your mother and I never really hit it off. Not from the moment that she clapped eyes on me, and me on her to be fair. Your Grandfather blamed it on post natal depression, but then he knew bugger all about anything, let alone the saturnine – or perhaps that should that be satanical - complexities of the female mind.

Truth be told, your mother was the most unappealing baby that was ever dragged kicking and screaming into this world. We were both screaming, which hardly bode well.

As for me, the way I looked and felt it would surely have been enough to scare the poor infant half to death. Herod's men had nothing on me. "Whatever", as you young people are want to say, neither of us ever recovered from that inauspicious beginning.

I think it unlikely that she would wish to touch a penny of mine. She actually told me so the last time we had the misfortune to meet – at your Uncle Gerry's funeral. And what a disaster that was, what with the funeral director insisting that your uncle's last wish to be cremated was observed, and your mother buying a plot anyway, and tipping his ashes straight into it because she had wanted him to be interred. It didn't help that she overheard your father observing that there was little point given that not only was there nothing left to raise on Judgement Day, but that Gerry had been a bigger atheist than Karl Marx.

You, on the other hand, have always seemed to have a soft spot for me, and I suppose that in responding to those early signs of wholly unselfish affection I was doing my best to compensate for my appalling parenting skills.

Anyway, I trust that you won't be silly and feel that you either have to decline, or share, your inheritance? You have made your own way in the world, against considerable odds, not least your own family, and I include myself in that. I know that you possess both the wisdom and the sensitivity to put it to good use. Far better than I, or your mother, might have done.

You will note that I have made a small number of other bequests. They may strike you, and others, as somewhat bizarre, but trust me they are the least I could do given the tenuous connections that they have to the late resurgence in my fame and fortune.

Please don't think too badly of me. I am what I am. Or should that be I was what I was? I believe that in a small way my novels brought momentary pleasure – or at the very least mental anaesthesia – to a considerable number of people. Not the most philanthropic endeavour in the world, but something at least.

I was, as you know, a fellow traveller of your uncle's in as much as I do not expect anyone of either gender to be waiting for me with a pair of scales and a big book in which are writ my many sins, and negligible charities. If there is, it will serve me right. Towards the end I surprised myself, though not as much I suspect as I may still surprise you.

As my only judge therefore, I hope that you will come - if not to forgive me – at least to retain one or two fond memories of the person that was,*

Your Loving (sic) Grandmother,

Charley

**If not, please feel free to you use your new found wealth to make amends. I shall be past caring!*

I placed the three sheets of paper back into the envelope, and put it in my handbag. There was a discreet knock on the door and Henry Frobisher, our family solicitor, popped his head around the door.

'Have you finished?' he asked.

'Yes thank you.'

'Good.'

He slid noiselessly into the room.

'It was marked confidential, so you don't need to tell me anything of course...unless it contains any instructions for me to act upon?'

I shook my head. 'No it doesn't.'

He tried a little too hard to hide his disappointment. It was only natural that he should be curious I suppose. He had known and worked for my mother for years.

'In which case,' he said, a little too brusquely for my liking. 'I think that's everything. As your grandmother's main beneficiary you are going to be a very wealthy young woman. Not that that's any consolation I'm sure,' he added hastily. 'If there is anything that Frobisher and Frobisher can do to assist you in the future you can rest assured that we would be honoured so to do.'

I bet you would, I thought. I just wanted to get out of there. My grandmother's letter had unsettled me. It was as though she had strewn clues and misdirections within it just as she had done in all of her novels. She was daring me to follow them, and solve the mystery. I had a pretty good idea where to start; the obituary for my Grandmother that I had only just read in the Guardian Review section

Unfortunately I had already consigned it to the mixed paper, cards, and cartons wheelie bin that the London Borough of Richmond upon Thames collection crew had emptied punctually the previous morning. No matter, a quick Google on my MacBook Air produced the following:

Guardian Online. November 18th 2011 Meabh O'Leary

Tributes poured in today for Charlotte "Charley" Webster, winner of the CWA Cartier Diamond Dagger for sustained excellence in crime writing, and one of the most popular and beloved writers of British crime fiction. Her first novel, T*he Angel in the Alley,* was regarded as perhaps the finest piece of crime fiction - in the Agatha Christie tradition - of the second half of the 20th Century. In 2012, just as it seemed that her muse might be failing her - and that she had fallen out of favour with her publishers - she burst back onto the literary scene with *The Readers*. This brilliant short story/novella, playful and sinister in turns, caught the imagination of the public, and became an overnight sensation. Not least, because she chose to publish it herself, first as an eBook, and then in a short story anthology in paperback. Nobody was more surprised than she when the eBook sales reached a million in the first month.

'This is a vindication...' she said at the time, '...of the reader as the one and only true arbiter of literary taste, and proof positive that there can be no substitute for hands on experience.'

What a tease she was! We shall miss you Charley. But your work lives on.

I must have been the only person not to have read *The Readers.* You see my grandmother and my mother had been estranged ever since she'd divorced my grandfather and had chosen to become something of a recluse. That had made it difficult for me to see her. Although I realise that now that was only an excuse. My life had taken a different direction, one that had led me abroad. Furthermore, I had literary ambitions of my own, and did not want to find myself comparing my writing with hers, or being accused of riding on her coat tails.

It was with a strange mixture of anticipation and regret that I powered up my Kindle, waited all of twenty seconds for the download to come through, and began to read.

The Readers
By
Charley Webster

If you want to blame someone, blame my agent. I do. It all started with a phone call.

'Charley, it's Hermione here. We need to talk.'

I could tell by the tone of her voice, and the sound bite sentence construction, that it was bad news. But the real clincher came next.

'Let's make it Costa Coffee, 2pm this afternoon. The one in New Oxford Street.'

If it had been good news she'd have gone for the Ritz, or The Savoy; Hermione's like that. Not that *I* have anything against Costa Coffee. Au contraire. But it wasn't even the one in Waterstone's, on Gower Street, just yards from her office. She didn't want us to be seen together. That bad.

'Have you heard from..?' I started to say, but she'd already ended the call. As it turned out she had.

'Alicia James, at Purposive Press,' she said, sipping her skinny latte through barely parted lips. The froth left a faint moustache that made her look ridiculous. 'And she was always such a fan of yours. A champion even. So disappointing.'

She was waiting for me to say something, but I wasn't going to make it easy for her. Only last week my accountant had pointed out that over the past twenty years Hermione, and the agency of which she was the founding partner, had earned – although that wasn't the word he chose to use – close to one and a half a million pounds from their percentage on my royalties and sale of foreign rights. Now that times were tough he wondered if perhaps she was giving up on me. It was a thought that had nagged away at me these last few months; one that I had resisted. Until now.

'What did she say?' I asked.

'She loved the setting. I quote: *It was clever of Charley to set such evil amidst a pastoral idyll so reminiscent of Thomas Hardy*. That was one of several aspects she thought original.'

'Several?'

'Well, there was your use of flash forwards where one might have expected flash backs. That really intrigued her.'

'And?'

'That was about it.' She started in on her vanilla iced cup cake.

'Was there anything she actually hated?' I prompted. 'You can tell me Hermione, you know I can handle criticism.'

She chomped away for a moment or two, subsiding into a studied mastication. I could tell she was playing for time. Trying to find a safe and kindly way to put it. Finally giving up.

'You should never have changed your protagonist.'

'On *your* advice!' I retorted. She raised one eyebrow. Whenever she did that it made me want to slap her face.

'Are you sure?'

'Positive.'

'Well it must have been something Alicia suggested. I wouldn't have sent you down that route willy nilly. Anyway, you shouldn't take it personally.'

Not take it personally? Did she think it was someone else's work being savaged here? Did she think I'd had it ghost written?

'I'm having the same problem with all of my longstanding clients,' she said.

There was rather too much emphasis on *problem,* and *long standing*.

'I'm sensing that there's a little more to it than that.' I said

She nodded sagely. 'They're looking for something fresh and new.'

'As opposed to old and tired?'

She pretended to not to have heard.

'The market's changed forever. Gone are the halcyon days of editors and agents working together to encourage, grow, and nurture new literary talent. The accountants are in charge. Fast bucks is the order of the day.'

'Shouldn't that be...*are the order,* or *are the orders*?' I said.

'Dumming down,' she hurried on. 'May equate to poor quality but it is also synonymous with mass market appeal. The mass market doesn't give a damn about literary merit. It's only interested in celebrity, and reality; the more salacious and miserable the better. Imagination is no longer *de rigueur*. I blame the demise of radio and the rise of television. And don't even think about mentioning the internet. And just in case you think this is all about you, *intermediation* is now a dirty word...a thing of the past. We live in an increasingly dis-intermediated world.'

'If I knew what the hell that was I might be able to respond.' I said.

'All those years ago, why did you come to me with *The Angel in the Alley*? I'll tell you why. Because you'd tried sending it direct to the publishers in the vain hope that someone would finally get to it before it sunk without trace into the slush pile. You wanted me to act as a broker between you and the publishers...because that's what we do. And when, by dint of much perspiration and personal connections hard earned over years ...'

'Of long lingering champagne fuelled lunches.' I reminded her.

'...we'd finally managed to place you, there was Alicia nudging you this way and that, cajoling and praising as you honed your oeuvre.'

'You make it sound distinctly smutty.' I said.

'And finally there was the publisher, the ultimate broker between you and your adoring public. Intermediaries, that's what we were. But now any self-deluded halfwit with an aspiration to become an author can do so without a single intervention from those of us skilled and experienced in the recognition of literary merit.'

'Is that such a bad thing?' I asked. That stopped her in her tracks. I'd only said it because she was making me feel combative. But, as you'll already have gathered, she wasn't exactly tuned into how I might be feeling. Her face was suddenly crimson, her chest puffed up with a huge intake of breath as she marshalled her defence.

'Not such a bad thing?! Have you heard of the internet? Have you been on YouTube, or MySpace, or Facebook? Of course you have you're on all of them yourself.'

'At your suggestion. And to be fair, they've been quite useful as marketing tools.'

'You're missing the point. Are you being deliberately naive or simply mischievous?'

'And your point is?'

'Everyone's a writer! Everyone's a bloody author. Everyone's a movie making, video blogging, twitter tweeting, media celebrity. Even my window cleaner!'

'Is that so bad?'

'You're repeating yourself.'

'Only because you did.' I knew I was beginning to sound petty, but you could hardly blame me. Hermione was past noticing.

'Do you realise that those slush piles I helped you to circumvent, they're back with a vengeance, only this time they're all on line? All you have to do is upload your worthless piece of infantile ravings...'

'*My* worthless piece of infantile ravings?!' I protested

'Not yours, obviously. Then all you have to do is invest every waking hour in social networking across those sites, with the simple message – you vote for mine and I'll vote for yours – and as the votes pile in, your novel rises to the top where an editor's assistant takes a cursory look at the quality of the prose, and a hard look at the number of votes, and hey presto – a star is born.'

'So it's like an X Factor for novelists?'

'Precisely!' She raised her eyes skywards in thanksgiving for the fact the penny had finally dropped.

'I rather like X Factor.' I replied.

'You wouldn't be so flippant if you were an established musician who had spent a lifetime honing your skills, building your customer base, only to have some Johnny-come-lately push you out of the charts. And that's exactly what's starting to happen to us.'

'Us?' I hadn't seen much evidence of Hermione honing her skills.

'And don't think you can sit on your laurels and maintain your current lifestyle on the royalties from your previous titles. If that turncoat Alicia and her ilk get their way, a year from now people will be downloading them for free, and that's you and me up the Swannee.'

'I read in the Guardian Review,' I said. 'That there is supposedly a close relationship between digital downloads and sales of print versions.'

'Close it may be, but miniscule. And face it darling, miniscule is hardly going to cover your champers bill.'

'You're the one that drinks champagne Hermione.' I told her tartly.' I'm teetotal, or had you forgotten?'

'Be that as is may,' she replied. Another face slapping trigger. 'You're going to have to do something about it.'

'Shouldn't that be we?' I asked. 'You're my agent. What are *you* going to do about it?'

She licked the index finger of her right hand, used it to pick the remaining crumbs of vanilla icing from her plate, and transferred them to her little pink tongue. For some reason it brought to mind the chameleon that decorated the cover of my fifth novel – *The Chameleon*. Stating the obvious I know but this was pre post modernism. Then she spoke, and I realised that it had actually been a premonition.

'To be brutally honest - and as a friend and your agent I'm sure you wouldn't expect anything other from me – I don't think there's any point in trying anywhere else. Not the major publishing houses anyway. I mean, if Alicia isn't going to run with it that would mean finding a new publisher, and as I've already explained that's a non starter, and as for trying lower down the food chain, I'd hate to see you end up as supermarket fodder.'

She could see I was speechless.

'Best to put it behind you, and start again,' she said. 'Why don't you try something completely different? Something that'll take them by surprise. Treat it like an adventure.'

She'd finally run out of steam and waited for me to say something. I made her wait. To be honest I didn't know what to say. 'I'll do that then.' I said at last. 'I might even enjoy it I suppose.'

'You're not fooling me Charley,' she said leaning forward in an attempt to simulate empathy.

'I know you're hurting inside. But remember what it says in the Koran.'

I stared her out. 'I can't say I know it by heart.' I said.

She placed a hand over mine and squeezed it gently, as one might an elderly relative on her death bed. 'This too will pass.'

But it didn't. It festered.

A new voice, celebrity, and reality, that's what I took away from our conversation, and that's what finally gave me the idea. I may be getting old in the tooth, not that there aren't plenty of crime fiction novelists much older than me, and some didn't even begin to become famous until late into their sixties and seventies – Andrea Camilleri, a particular favourite of mine for one - but I am still something of a celebrity. No longer enough to guarantee publication clearly, but I do have a following.

As for reality, authenticity has always been something I've striven for. Why else those hours spent in pathology labs, attending post mortems, coroner's courts, and crown courts. Hanging out in pubs frequented by the criminal fraternity and detectives, sometimes ones where both are known to congregate. Pestering forensic psychiatrists and Googling late into the night. Never quite getting there because, as I'm sure you've discovered, reality *is* stranger than fiction.

Many a time I've discounted a plot because I thought it too fanciful, barbaric, unimaginably inhuman, only to turn on the television, pick up a paper, catch sight of the internet news, and find that someone has managed to go even further. Ten years ago I set up a folder on my computer called *Stranger than Fiction*. Into it I've copied every news story that beggared belief. To date it contains three thousand one hundred and seventy four such stories. That's almost one a day, and counting. So there was my challenge. How to compete with reality. Better still, how to *do* reality. And that's when it all came together. Bear with me. You'll see what I mean.

'How do you get inside the mind of a killer?' That's a question that regularly crops up at book launches, signings, and Q and A's. Sometimes they even have the grace to add '...so convincingly?'

My usual response has been about masses of research, reading biographies and autobiographies of killers, psychiatric tomes on the mind of the serial killer, case histories and so on. All of it true of course. But the other truth I've never revealed – not even to myself until quite recently – is that I've always found it rather easy. Worryingly so.

Not that I've ever felt the urge to act on those impulses you understand.

Not until now.

I have always researched my novels thoroughly, but this one required a great deal more attention to detail, as I'm sure you will come to understand in the fullness of time.

As I write this, there are over one thousand four hundred and thirty three unsolved murders in the UK, not counting over one thousand five hundred committed in Northern Ireland during what are rather euphemistically described as *The Troubles*. Those statistics do rather suggest that there may be such a thing as the perfect crime after all.

Most people seem to think that's about one's choice of modus operandi. There is something in that, but for my purposes the key was in selecting the perfect victim, or, to be more precise, victims.

I began by compiling a list of the qualities that I was looking for. They needed to be avid readers of crime fiction, with strong opinions and the willingness and ability to provide perceptive and useful feedback. It goes without saying that they would have to be living alone, and with no close relatives, friends, or nosy neighbours. Finally, and most important of all, they must have no prior connection to me, other than possibly having read one or more of my novels.

Not such a demanding list you may think. In reality, and remember that reality was what I was engaged in here, it proved surprisingly difficult.

The first obstacle I had to surmount was finding a way in which to meet my potential victims without arousing suspicion. It occurred to me that the many online communities built around books might be a perfect place to start. Here was a readymade source of avid readers, passionately committed to sharing their latest treasures and their pearls of literary wisdom with each other. A bit like a bloodless social network version of Pirates of the Caribbean.

I began by immersing myself in Goodreads, Reader2, BookTribes, Shelfari, YouWriteOn, Authonomy, and all the other related dotcoms. I had no idea there were so many. At first I found myself seduced into reading what the members of each site had to say about my own work. You have no idea how seductive and at times depressing that can become. A regular sadomasochistic enterprise, only without the erotic payoff normally associated with such activities. Or so I'm told.

Then I realised that this approach was fatally flawed. Whilst matching my first criterion one hundred percent, it made a mockery of my second. Far from being isolated and lonely, these folk were intimately connected with thousands of others. The clue was in the name, social network. How could I possibly have overlooked that little detail? It didn't bode well. In any case, even if I had been able to identify a lonely soul or two among these bustling virtual worlds, it was ten to a penny that my online registration, pattern of searches, and messages left to contact and entice them, would have left a data trail that a modern five year old, or *screen-ager* as Hermione is wont to call them, could follow.

There was nothing for it. I had to resort to good old traditional methods. What I asked myself would the serial killer do? It was a rhetorical question of course. After researching and writing thirty three murder mysteries I believed that I knew more about serial killers than your average senior investigating officer.

I had already classified my target population. Next I must identify where I would be most likely to find them. Then I had to ensure that I could observe, and eventually make contact with them, without arousing suspicion, or leaving evidence that might later incriminate me.

The answer was staring me in the face. The high street. Or to be precise, a number of high streets. For I would not be falling into the trap of common spatial location. My victims would be spread far and wide. In terms of their own geographical location that is, rather than their body parts. Even I have some qualms as you will have noticed from my avoidance of anything approaching *noir* in my novels.

I decided to begin where my love of reading had first been nurtured. Foyles Bookshop on the edge of Soho. It had the added attraction of being ten miles, yet only twenty minutes on the tube, from my home. Not during rush hour obviously. I alighted at Tottenham Court Road, only to discover that Crossrail had boarded up the entire block and I was forced to take a diversion around Centre Point in order to regain the Charing Cross Road.

I caught myself subconsciously seeking out CCTV cameras along the route, and had to force myself to behave as normally as possible. I had already decided to askew disguise of any kind. After all, I was well known at Foyles having been a customer since my ninth birthday. Furthermore, over thirty years of authorship various photographs on back covers, fly sheets, and posters in the windows, had charted the cruel and inexorable march of time across my face. It is the unexpected, the uncomfortable, the out of place, which detectives search for as they scrutinise the footage captured at, near, and to and from, the scene of crime.

I spotted her browsing in the crime fiction section. She was in her mid seventies, of average height, and average build, dressed in a beige tweed suit, with sensible, brown, flat heeled shoes. She had her back to me, her profile hidden by a mass of tight, mousey coloured curls.

What drew me to her was her total lack of presence, of individuality. She merged with her surroundings in the way that chameleons are said to do. As people brushed by she shrank a little, wearing her shyness like a carapace.

I watched her linger over Donna Leon's *Wilful Behaviour*, briefly consider Nesbo's *Nemesis*, before dropping it like a red hot coal, and finally settle on *The Given Day* by Dennis Lehane.

I followed her to the cafe, where she bought a filter coffee and a Chelsea bun. I chose a piece of vegan carrot cake, and a cup of tea. The place was packed of course, it always is. She stood there, the book under her arm, the mug of coffee in one hand and the plate with the bun in the other, indecision oozing painfully from every pore. To my right a couple made to leave. I tapped her lightly on the shoulder, causing her to jump like a startled rabbit.

'Over here.' I said, making for the table and standing guard while the former occupants squeezed themselves out from between the rustic wooden table and their chairs.

She regarded me with suspicion and uncertainty.

'It's OK,' I said reassuringly. 'There's nowhere else is there?'

She looked around in the vain hope that I might be wrong. After an excruciating pause, she finally capitulated, and came to join me.

'Thank you,' she whispered.

'You're welcome,' I said.

I pretended to stare out of the window, leaving her undisturbed to read the book, and sip her coffee though tightly pursed lips. A good ten minutes had passed before I leant forward and said.

'What do you think?'

She pretended not to have heard. I repeated myself a little louder this time.

'What do you think? About your book?'

For a moment I thought she might push back her chair and make her escape, but she was so tightly wedged in by the man behind her engrossed in his iPad that she couldn't have even if she'd wanted to. Nor did she have the courage to ask him to hitch up and make some room. She lowered her book and peered nervously over the top.

'It's...alright I suppose,' she said. 'Not what I was expecting.'

'I know,' I replied. 'All that stuff about Babe Ruth. It's hardly *Gone Baby Gone*, or *Mystic River*. But I think you should persevere. It soon picks up.'

She lowered it a fraction more.

'Really?'

'Yes, really,' I said. 'It's one of my favourites of his. A sort of a cross between *The Gangs of New York* and *The Naked City.*' I pointed to the cover. *'Epic, Enthralling, Powerful, Wrenchingly suspenseful...* It's not often that I concur with the critics but I have to say that for once I agreed with them.'

She placed the book down on the table.

'Really?'

'Yes, really.'

She attempted something approximating a smile. That was the moment I knew that I had her.

We spent a pleasant half an hour discussing favourite books that we had in common, she becoming quite animated at times. I bought her another coffee, and myself an Earl Grey, and it was only then that I dropped the bombshell.

'To be honest,' I said, 'It's refreshing to hear someone else's opinions. As a writer myself I find it hard to remain objective.'

She put down her mug, and stared at me.

'I knew I'd seen you somewhere before,' she squealed. 'No. Don't tell me. You're...you're Shirley...Chelsea...'

'Charley?' I suggested helpfully.

'That's it!' she exclaimed. 'Charley Webster! You're Charley Webster. Oh My...God!'

All this with such X Factor enthusiasm that heads were beginning to turn. Not what I wanted at all.

She took a deep breath before lowering her voice and hurrying on. 'But I love your work. I've read them all you know. My God! Charley Webster. I don't believe it.'

Such was her unalloyed delight that, when it came, she seized my proposal like manna from heaven.

'But of course I will,' she said. 'I'd loved to. It'll be an honour, and a privilege.'

'There are rules,' I told her. 'Strict rules. I'm going to send you random chapters, partly because I don't want to spoil it for you when the book comes out, and partly because I wouldn't want the whole thing to fall into the wrong hands. It has happened before.'

Her eyes widened with shock and alarm.

'Surely not?'

'Oh, yes,' I said. 'But it's far too painful to talk about.'

'I understand.'

She reached out her hand intending to close it over mine, but I withdrew it with the pretext of picking up my cup. The last thing I wanted was physical contact. Nothing to do with DNA you understand, it was just that I had no intention of becoming emotionally involved.

'Secondly, and most importantly, you must promise not to breathe a word of this to anyone. Nor to write anything about it – other than your critique for me – and certainly not to blog, text, tweet or Facebook anything, however slight, about our agreement.'

'Fat chance,' she said. 'I have no one to tell, and as for all those techie things I don't even own a computer or a mobile phone.'

I had already checked this out by dint of casual

conversation. Not only was she friendless, but as an only child, and a childless widow of ten years standing, there was no family either.

'Jolly good,' I said. 'In that case all I need is your address. Then, when the book is written – it'll take about five months I'm afraid because I've some more research to do - I'll send you the relevant chapters. I'll give you a fortnight to review them, then I'll give you a ring to see if you're ready for me to come over.'

'Why don't I ring you?'

'No,' I said, a little too firmly. '*I* shall ring *you*.'

We parted the best of friends, and co-conspirators, she with a spring in her step, and *The Given Day* tucked under her arm. Such was her excitement that she nearly forgot to pay for it. I made sure that she did. I didn't want them trawling the CCTV this early in the game.

I waited a respectable ten minutes before I followed. The address she had given me was across town. Somewhere in that triangle between the Westway, The Edgware Road, and Bayswater Road. I could of course be more precise but you wouldn't want me to make it too easy for you would you?

Reasoning that Hannah, for such was her name, *not her real name obviously*, would probably take the Tube, I took the bus, alighting several blocks away from where the A to Z informed me that she lived. I had decided to come at it from several directions, one at a time naturally, not all at once, that would have been silly, not to mention impossible.

The first route I chose, peppered with cameras, was a complete non starter. On one particular corner there was a great monstrosity of a thing such as one observes on particularly vulnerable car parks. A great glass globe atop a long black pole painted with that anti vandal stuff that's supposed to make it impossible to climb. Only this one was outside a pub come wine bar. No surprise there I thought. Almost immediately opposite this the hospital walls – bit of a giveaway I know but let's face it you're not really going to take this seriously, or at least I hope not – had a whole string cameras on them. What were they expecting a drugs raid?

The second route I chose was much better. Once I'd got off the main drag there was this lovely street lined with Georgian terraces and mews. A patch of green at one end, a former church, and a few more salubrious commercial premises. Two of them – very close to the address in question – did have cameras on them but they were angled downwards towards the parking spaces more concerned with capturing illegal parkers, and TWOCers, than your average passer-by.

Note: Those of you familiar with my novels will know that TWOC is an acronym used by police and other law enforcement agencies to refer to persons *taking without the owner's consent.*

Hannah's address turned out to be a basement flat surrounded by black wrought iron railings, and with a series of steps leading down to an anonymous front door. Just perfect. There would be no need to seek entry through the front door at street level, and run the risk of bumping into sundry occupants of the other flats. It would take only a second to slip down the steps and out of sight, and remain so whilst waiting for the door to open. On leaving I would pop my head above the parapet to make sure that the street was empty before mounting the steps and walking the twenty meters or so to the main road, and off into the night.

Four months later, almost to the day, I rang her in the morning from a phone box a week before the date on which I intended to call. A sensible precaution in the unlikely event that the police might check her phone records.

Hannah was beside herself with excitement. Not that that meant much, only that there was every possibility of her expiring from a coronary before I could get to her.

We arranged that I should call at seven thirty in the evening. She wanted to make dinner but I told her that I would already have eaten and would have to be away by eight thirty.

I had originally intended to use succinylcholine, a colourless and virtually untraceable drug, resulting in rapid onset paralysis, and death from asphyxiation and/or cardiac arrest. However, my brief affair with a consultant anaesthetist took a nasty turn when he was caught removing drugs for his own personal use – a practice which I was hoping I could use as a lever to induce him to provide me with a supply of succinylcholine. On the up side, I would have had to inject the drug into the victims – any muscle would have done – which would have meant selecting either diabetics or drug users, for fear of the tell tale pin prick mark alerting the pathologist.

In the case of the first I would have found it morally abhorrent, and time consuming, not to mention a bit of a giveaway if some over enthusiastic detective inspector decided to enter "diabetes" into the search field of HOLMES. [That's the Home Office Large Major Enquiry System in case you haven't got round to reading *A Fatal Intervention*. The "Large" has always struck me as somewhat superfluous given that it's immediately followed by "Major". But that's what happens when PC Plod and computer geeks put their heads together.]

As for targeting drug users, I would have stuck out

like a sore thumb around their haunts, and the last thing I needed was a needle stick injury from an HIV or hepatitis B carrier.

In the end I plumped for a tropane alkaloid plant derivative. Much more accessible. Colourless, tasteless, odourless, and undetectable without specific tests designed to look for it, and only then by identifying minute changes in the haemoglobin within the red blood cells. Since the effect of this particular poison is to cause cardiac arrest and, given the age and nervous disposition of my victims, the likelihood of the attending physician or the pathologist having their suspicions aroused was in my view miniscule. And when was any worthwhile endeavour devoid of risk?

You're not expecting me to name the substance surely? That would be so irresponsible. Suffice it to say that it is a poison well known to crime writers, and about which there is copious information on the internet. Incidentally, it has the added advantage of being fast acting, thus eliminating the possibility of the victim resisting, hurting herself, or calling for help.

The street was lined with cars parked up in the residents' bays. Flakes of snow fell softly from an ink black sky, caught in the beam of a sodium street lamp as they fluttered by. I had judged that at this time on a cold winter's evening most people would be home eating their dinner in front of a wood burning store. Anyone still abroad would hardly notice the middle aged woman walking down the centre of the street, wrapped up against the cold, a scarf across her face, and her bowed head hidden by the hood of her coat.

There was no one to be seen as I stepped back onto the pavement, opened the gate, and carefully negotiated steps slick with a fine white coat of snow.

I stood before a royal blue painted door, that had a

brass knocker, and a cheerful Xmas wreath of holly and ivy tied up with a tartan bow. This was the point of no return.

I felt, with fingers covered by a black leather glove, for the vial in my left coat pocket, took a deep breath, exhaled slowly, and knocked.

The door flew open. The woman I had come to know as Hannah stood there beaming a broad smile of which I would never have thought her capable.

'Charley!' she exclaimed as though taken by surprise. 'You came? I wasn't sure that you would.' She stepped to one side and gestured down the hallway. 'Come in, come in.'

I wiped my feet on the mat, waited for her to close the door, and then followed her along the light oak lined passage to the lounge.

It was a cosy little room with a two seater regency style sofa and matching single armchair, both covered in a fading beige floral fabric.

'Let me take your coat and scarf,' she said holding out her hands.

'If it's alright with you,' I replied. 'I'd rather keep them on for a moment. Until I am somewhat acclimatised.'

If I had to leave traces – and everybody does – I'd rather control exactly what and where they were.

'Of course,' she said, a little flustered that I'd knocked her off her stride. 'But you must let me get you a cup of tea. Earl Grey isn't it?'

'You remembered?' I said. 'How kind.'

I sat down on the sofa, with my handbag beside me, as she scurried off into the kitchen where I could hear her busying herself with cups and saucers. I used the time to look around the room.

A simulated coal fire powered by gas provided heat and warmth. An artificial Christmas tree in the corner appeared to be the only sign that this was a festive season. Plain gold curtains were drawn in the small bay window, in front of which stood a television on a stand. There was no sign of a DVD or tape recorder/player. On the period mantelpiece, where Christmas cards might otherwise have stood, was a black and white photograph of a much younger version of her, in a '50s post war wedding dress, staring into the eyes of her handsome dark haired groom. Beside the photo stood a carriage clock, with a small brass pendulum, that punctuated the silence with a dull tick tock marking the seconds lost forever.

It was a sad room that spoke of a solitary life. A life without meaning, purpose, or direction. An existence bounded by memories, suspended between life and death. It put me in mind of the Latin epigraph to T S Eliot's *The Waste Land,* in which he quoted from the Satyricon of Petronius:

"For I myself once saw with my own eyes the Sibyl hanging in her jar, and when the boys asked her, 'Sibyl, what do you want?' she answered 'I want to die.'"

On the glass topped coffee table lay the pages I had sent her. She saw me looking down at them as she entered the room carrying a loaded tray.

'Just wonderful,' she gushed. 'I loved them. So intriguing.'

She nudged them to one side to make room for the tray, and placed it carefully down. There were two plain white china cups and saucers with a pretty hand painted fuchsia flower decoration, a matching teapot, a plain white milk jug, a sugar bowl, and a plate of dark chocolate digestive biscuits.

She sat down in the armchair, perched on the edge of the seat, her cup and saucer balanced on her knees. She leaned forward expectantly, watching as I blew across the surface of my tea, and took a sip.

'How is it?' she asked nervously.

'Superb,' I told her. And it was.

'I bought it in specially, from Postcard Teas,' she said.

No wonder then. That delicious little blue fronted shop in the former Victorian grocery store off New Bond Street, where tea had been sold for over two hundred years. Straight out of a Dickens' novel I'd thought the first time Hermione had taken me there. It must have cost poor Hannah half her pension to buy this tea for me.

'I've written down my thoughts as you asked me to.' She nodded towards the sheaf of papers in front of me. 'But I expect you'd like to hear them from the horse's mouth as it were?'

She giggled nervously at that, causing her hands to shake, slopping some of the pale brown liquid over the side of her cup.

'Oh, look at me!' she said, placing the cup on the floor beside her chair and hurrying off into the kitchen, returning with some poly roll to dab it up. As she sat down she caught me staring at the photograph on the mantelpiece.

'You made a perfect couple.' I said.

She smiled wistfully. 'We were. Harold was a wonderful man. He was in the London Fire Brigade you know.'

I let her witter on, about how they had met at the Hammersmith Palais, about their early years of struggle during the post war years, about their deep disappointment of discovering that she would never be able to give birth. The gradual coming to terms with a life as a childless couple. A comfortable middle age, and then the sudden, cruel, devastating knock on the door. The kindly policewoman who told her how Harold had had a massive heart attack whilst fighting a fire in Camden Town.

'Dead on arrival. He would have felt nothing.'

Maybe not, but all the feeling was left for her to suffer.

'It was April the First,' she said. 'April Fool's Day. Easy to remember...not that I'd ever forget.'

Elliot again, I reflected. For Hannah at least, April was indeed the cruellest month.

'Do you miss him a lot?' I asked.

A stupid question I know, but it had to be asked. I suppose a proper sociopath would not have cared one way or another. But then what is a real sociopath? Can there be such a thing as an improper sociopath? A sociopath in the making?

She turned to look at the photograph. 'More than you could possibly imagine.'

In the silence that followed, perturbed only by the ticking and the tocking of the clock, I felt a sense of vindication.

'So,' I said at last. 'What did you really think?'

Awoken from her reverie she turned and smiled wanly.

'As I said, I loved it. It's difficult sometimes when you only have a few pages to go at, but in this case it made it all the more intriguing.'

'Go on.'

'Well, when your protagonist turned up at the home of that burnt out executive alcoholic spinster in Newcastle; I sensed immediately that there was something sinister going on. The same with the battered wife who'd left her husband and changed her name.'

She paused as though expecting me to comment. When I didn't, she soldiered on.

'You don't have to tell me if you don't want to, but

I got the distinct impression that she was going to do them in. You know...murder them. But I haven't yet worked out why.'

'Maybe *she* hasn't yet worked out why?' I said.

She thought about that, and then she shook her head earnestly.

'Oh no, I'm sure she knows. Well, I'm sure *you* know, which must mean that she will, eventually. This incidentally, would make her the perpetrator rather than the protagonist.' She said that as though it had only just occurred to her.

'What about the language, how did that strike you?' I asked.

'Oh wonderful, as ever. Lots of irony, hardly any cliché, realistic dialogue, lots of foreshadowing, appropriate point of view, and lovely character development – as far as I could tell from such short passages. Typically you in fact.'

'And the settings?' I said. 'You haven't mentioned the settings.'

Her brow furrowed slightly and I could tell that she was searching for the right words.'

'Well...'

'Go on Hannah,' I said. 'You can tell me, I've got broad shoulders.'

Not true on either count. My shoulders are actually quite narrow, thus accentuating the pear shape that has plagued me all my life. And I haven't yet met an author who really relishes criticism of the work over which they've struggled long and hard, even if they do grin and bear it.

'Well, that's the one area I think you might want to have another look at,' she said, beginning to make it easier for me. 'It's probably just me, but I thought there was just a little *too* much detail in your description of the towns she arrived at, and the homes in which the readers lived. I thought it distracted one somewhat from the characters themselves. And then there's the issue of *pace...*'

She was really warming to her subject now, digging herself deeper.

'...it did tend to flag, I found, when the readers began to feed back to her. Take Muriel's for example.'

She put her cup down and reached across to rifle through the sheets of paper. She pulled one out and held it up triumphantly. It was only then that I noticed the copious pencil marks in the margins and between the double spaced lines. My, I thought, you've really gone to town.

I won't bore you with the details, partly because I found them painful, but also because I have decided to take her advice. You don't need to hear all their feedback, even if I did. I waited until she'd run out of steam, then I said.

'That's so illuminating dear, and *so* helpful. I wonder, could I have a glass of water?

While she was out of the room I slipped the vial from my pocket, emptied the contents into her cup, and then topped it up from the pot.

'I took the liberty of topping you up,' I said as she handed me the glass. ''You'd let it get cold.'

'You're so thoughtful,' she said sitting down, and picking up her cup and saucer.

In the event, it took a little longer than I had anticipated. Twenty two minutes to be precise. A definite flush appeared on her cheeks, and I could see the carotid artery on her neck throbbing in time with her racing pulse. The plate she was holding slipped from her fingers, and fell to the floor. She attempted to pick it up her but it was clear that her vision was blurred. She over-reached, and toppled from the chair onto the parquet boards.

I stood up, crossed behind the furthest edge of the coffee table, and knelt beside her. I was briefly tempted to move her into the recovery position, but how would that have been interpreted by the police? As it was, her knees tucked up in a foetal position under their own steam as the muscles began to spasm.

I stood up and collected my cup, saucer, plate, and glass, and took them into the kitchen where I washed and dried them, found the cupboards in which they belonged, and put them away. Then I took one of the plastic sandwich bags I had brought with me from my pocket, and emptied into it half of the used tea leaves from the stainless steel infuser on the drainer.

When I returned she was unconscious. Still alive, but only just. I gathered up the sheets of paper, encircled them with an elastic band, and placed them in the inside pocket of my coat. Then I took from my handbag a pair of polyethylene disposable over shoes I'd bought from an online decorating supplies company, and made my way back down the hall to her bedroom. A careful search confirmed that there was nothing there that could link her to me.

The second bedroom was another matter entirely. She had converted it into a sort of study come reading room. A six shelf oaken bookcase took up half of one wall. Against another was a desk, such as one might find in IKEA, on which stood six neat box files where she kept her letters and accounts. Three plastic tubs contained her biros, pen, pencils, rubber, Pritt stick, and a pair of scissors. Three drawers contained A4 notebooks, A4 pads, scrap paper, and a calculator.

On the desk lay an A4 pad from which sheets had been removed. I held it at an angle to the light, relieved that the curtains had been drawn before I arrived. Sure enough, there were indentations. Faint but discernible. It was impossible to tell if this was the pad from which the sheets in my pocket had been torn, but either way, forensic examination would certainly have revealed what had been written. I tore the next five pages from the pad, folded them, and placed them with the others in my coat.

I turned my attention to the book case. It was crammed full of books. Two deep on four of the shelves. One shelf was dedicated to books on London, including Ackroyd's *London The Biography,* and Mayhew's *London.* The majority were of the crime fiction genre. At head height, on the centre shelf, the entire collected works of Charlotte Webster held pride of place.

For a moment I considered removing them, on the basis that since my novels were likely to feature in every one of my victim's homes this might be a common element that would lead to my door. Commonsense prevailed, though it could just as easily have been pride. I convinced myself that since my victims homes would be hundreds of miles apart, and the likelihood that a list of the entire collection of novels in each of them would be entered into the Holmes database, when natural causes was the obvious diagnosis, was close to zero, it was unnecessary.

Something was missing though. Something that should have been either here or in the bedroom. I was damned if I knew what it was. I made a cursory search of the bathroom and retraced my steps to the lounge.

Hannah had gone. Not physically, not her actual body, that would have been silly not to mention disastrous, but her soul had gone to join her beloved Harold.

I found the broom cupboard under the stairs, and brought out the little Dyson hoover, and the duster mop she must have used to polish the floors and proceeded to hoover everywhere that I had been.

I was just about to pull the kitchen door too behind me when I spotted it. Hanging from a peg on the wall, to the side of the refrigerator, was a calendar. The kind that comes free from a certain well known charity in the hope that it will elicit a one off charitable donation, or even the setting up of a direct debit. On there, there against that day's date, she had written a reminder:

Get McVitie's Chocolate Digestives for CW this aft.

So much for our agreement! Hannah had broken the rules. A surge of anger swept through me. If she had not already been dead I could have killed her.

I was in a quandary. What to do next? If I left it there the police would surely want to find this mysterious CW. It would not take a genius to link that to my novels on that bookcase upstairs. On the other hand, if I took down the calendar someone would surely wonder why she didn't have one in the house. In the end I had no option. The books were too bulky to take with me, and in any case if they looked into her habits and visited Foyles asking about possible CWs, someone might recall her having shouting my name.

I took down the calendar, shoved it in my pocket, which by now was beginning to bulge, and replaced it with a tea towel that was hanging over the cooker rail. Then I took a paper bag from the dispenser hanging in the broom cupboard, placed it in the sink, and carefully emptied the hoover compartment into the bag. Then, grateful that the hoover had recently been emptied, I rolled the bag into the smallest size I could manage, tied it tightly, and stuffed it into the remaining space in my copious handbag. Then I searched the cupboards until I found a half empty packet of sea salt. I emptied it into a piece of polyroll which I scrunched into a ball in my left hand.

That done, I put the hoover and the floor duster

away, walked to the front door, and turned out the hallway light.

I slowly counted to one hundred, using the rhythm to slow the beat of my heart, clasped the handle, turned the Yale catch, pulled up my hood, wrapped my scarf tighter, and opened the door a fraction.

The snow was falling faster now and lay an inch thick on the steps. I opened the door a little wider, stepped out into the stairwell, and pulled the door shut behind me.

I moved with a shuffling action up the steps, conscious that I still wore my over shoes and they had little or no grip on the surface. When my eyes were level with the pavement I scanned the street as far as I could see. It was empty. I bent to remove the over shoes and pushed them up my left sleeve. Then I unwrapped the polyroll and, as I backed up the stairs with the same shuffling motion, began to sprinkle the salt where my feet had trod, all the way to the far edge of the pavement.

Then I stepped into the road and headed off in the tyre tracks, towards the main road.

There is a general convention among crime writers that the perpetrator finds his or her first murder the hardest, both emotionally, and when it comes to planning. Well maybe not emotionally, at least not for the sociopath, but in terms of the amount of stress it generates. I can't say I found it so.

The others were all much of a muchness. In terms of execution that is. I honed my skills a little but by and large I think I pretty much nailed it that first time. Except that, apart from meeting my essential criteria, the contexts and characters of my victims differed widely.

There was, for example, the second time around

divorcee in Hull, estranged from both her former husbands, and so bitter and disillusioned that she spurned men forevermore. The burnt out alcoholic spinster in Manchester – yes funny I know but I did actually find one, not where I'd written her to be when I started out, but there you are. And there was also, just as I had predicted, a victim of domestic violence who had been re-housed by the council and been so scared of her partner that she had lived a life of total anonymity ever since. And the woman from Bristol who had spent a decade caring for her demented - literally that is not figuratively – husband.

I like to think that I released them all from a slow, sad, depressing journey into oblivion. But that's probably a post hoc rationalisation as Sister Bernadette my former History teacher was wont to say.

I owe them a debt that I can never repay. Apart from providing the subject matter for this story, the feedback that they provided was more perceptive and useful than any I have received, including from Hermione and my various Editors. It is possible I suppose that I only think that because the fate I had in store for each of my Readers gave me a moral obligation to take what they had to say seriously.

Either way, they really helped to shape this story, and will continue to inform my subsequent writing. So, if this story isn't for you, you know who to blame.

What is it they say about killing the goose that lays the golden egg? It isn't really a problem I discovered, so long as you make sure they've laid the egg first.

*****

It was only when I'd finished reading that I realised that I had not paused long enough to take a single sip of my gin and tonic. I picked up the glass, raised it to my lips, and downed the contents in one.

Charley's story was exactly as Meabh O'Reilly of The Guardian had described it. Playful and sinister by turns. Taken at face value – just another fantastical imagining of a cynical writer of crime fiction – it was at worst a mischievous dig at the world of publishing, and Charley herself. It was also an interesting reflection on the fine line that divides those who can imagine committing a crime, and those who actually commit one.

Seen through the lens of the letter that she had written to me, and taking into account what I recalled of the bequests she had made in her will, an altogether more sinister interpretation sprang to mind.

I got up, walked into my study, and opened the draw in the beechwood filing cabinet marked *C W - Matters Pertaining To.* I took out the buff envelope containing Charley's will. I took it back into the lounge, topped up my G&T, and homed in on the relevant section –*Bequests*.

There were five altogether – excluding mine - each of £100,000. The charities concerned were the Greater London Fire Service Benevolent Fund, The World Wild Life Fund, The Samaritans, The Alzheimer Carers' Association, and Shelter.

So I was right. Either Charley was settling a debt she felt she owed to her imaginary victims because of the resurgence in her career that they had helped to bring about...or...

Either way, I had to know. I downed my second gin and tonic, booted up my iPad, and opened Google Earth.

It's amazing what you can accomplish with Google Earth in *Street View* mode. Especially in London where every street is covered. But in the end it all comes down to wearing out the shoe leather. Or in my case, the EVA soles of my best Ugg boots.

I had narrowed the search area down to a small cluster of three streets within the triangle Charley had so sportingly described. I had the advantage of going in daylight, and it took less than fifteen minutes for me to strike gold.

At the junction of Praed Street with Norfolk Place I found the imposing arch and black wrought iron gates of St Mary's Hospital. Immediately opposite, straddling the corner, stood No 109, otherwise known as Fountains Abbey. A glorious Victorian Public house offering, among other delicacies, traditional bangers and mash, cask ales, and linguine pesto. Right outside the door, from a tall black pole, hung the pictorial pub sign, and biggest top hat globe lamp I had ever seen.

I set off down Norfolk Place, my hands and feet tingling with anticipation. I took the second left into Star Street. Stopping for a moment, I glanced back down the street and saw the stretch of greenery that I knew marked Norfolk Square. I carried on, passing in front of a high brick wall lined by seven plane trees and, just visible beyond the last of them, a monstrous orange face with protruding eyes –one sightless - painted on the side of the end terrace.

It was just as she'd described. Row upon row of neat Georgian terraced houses, comprising a basement, ground floor, and two floors above. Original sash windows. Neatly painted front doors in red, and blue and green. Close by, two commercial premises, one each side of the street, were watched over by pairs of boxy cameras focused solely on the entrances and parking spaces.

The number I had found in grandma's address book corresponded with a basement flat surrounded by railings, and with red geraniums in the window box of the flat above.

I rang the bell on the pretext of enquiring about an elderly great aunt who I had been led to believe lived here, but there was no answer. I felt foolish and conspicuous standing on the pavement outside, so I resolved to return that evening. As I made my way down towards the London Road, I saw the postman coming towards me. I retraced my steps, and waited outside the flat.

He had letters and circulars for the main house, but none for the flat. When he'd finished popping them through the letterbox I started my spiel.

'Sorry,' he said. 'There's no-one of that description living here. Although I believe the former occupant was an elderly woman. I never met her, because I only started delivering here six years ago.'

He started to go, then paused and turned back.

'But I do recall the estate agent at No 27 saying something about having a devil of a time getting rid of it. In probate for several years apparently, because they couldn't find a will or a surviving relative. Sad when you think about it.'

I resumed my walk up to the junction with the Edgeware Road where, whilst trying to gather my thoughts, something caught my eye in the window of Lloyds Bank. An old milestone, with a plaque beside it. I bent to read it.

This milestone marked the distance to Tyburn Gate and The Gallows where over 50,000 people were hung in the 500 years up to 1783 when it was finally demolished.

I wondered if this was yet another of Charley's clues,

or simply a co-incidence. And then I remembered. She had mentioned Peter Ackroyd's *London* on a bookshelf in the study of her first victim. The one outside whose flat I had been standing moments before.

I found the reference I was looking for on page three hundred and two. Ackroyd spoke of it as one of London's mysteries. Apparently there was a superstition that if one dreamt of the gallows then good fortune would come one's way. Well in my grandmother's case it certainly had, though whether she had dreamt of the gallows or not, we would never know.

I could have probed a little further, but what was the point? What was I proposing to do if my suspicions turned out to be well founded? Grass up my Grandmother? To what effect exactly? The police investigation would cost a heap of money and, with no one to prosecute, the CPS would be unlikely to want to take it any further. It would sully her memory, and infuriate her millions of fans. On whom would they vent their spleen? Little old me, that's who. I might just as well brand myself a Holocaust denier. In any case, I had no proof. Nor would there ever be any after all this time.

And who was to say that this was not a figment of her imagination constructed around real people. Women she had come across in reading groups, meet-the-author events, at book signings, or in Waterstone's cafes. She could easily have elided these living and breathing people with other women whose deaths she had found recorded in local newspapers. It was the kind of literary conceit in which she delighted. The Guardian had it right; as far back as I remembered she had always been a tease.

So, I resolved to leave it there. Not to forget it exactly, because that wasn't going to happen. And in any case, it had served as something of an inspiration. I had a book to write and, thanks to Charley, the wherewithal to publish it myself. Not that I needed the money. But I did deserve the recognition, the respect, and the sense of achievement. And, after all those wasted years, those cruel rejections, I knew exactly what I was going to do. I suspect that Charley had known when she decided to sit down and write that letter. I suppose it's in the genes.

That evening, armed with a white wine spritzer, I opened a new document in Word, and began to type.

The Publishers
By
Alice Webster

Chapter 1
Rejection

To Die For

Something had woken her. Melissa felt sure of that. She sat up wearily, and checked the bedside alarm. The eerie green display said 3.59am.

She listened for a moment, and then sunk back onto the pillows. It would be because Mike was away. She often found in difficult to sleep when he was out of town.

There was a scraping noise from the room below. She sat bolt upright, fists clenching the duvet to her chest.

She cursed herself for forgetting to set the alarm before she'd come up to bed. That was Mike's job. He'd told her over and over again how important it was that she didn't forget when he wasn't there to do it.

There it was again. Someone was moving the furniture. Now there was the sound of a sash window in the lounge being opened. Unthinking, she went to the bedroom window, pushed back the curtain, and pulled on the sash. As the window rose she craned her head and shoulders out.

In the soft orange glow of the sodium street lamp she saw immediately beneath her a bundle of some kind tied with strips of wide black tape. Beside it, half in shadow, someone was leaning back across the window sill, reaching into the room. A man, she felt sure of it. She wanted to shout for help but fear had closed her throat like a vice. He backed out of the shadow of the house and straightened up. In his right hand he clutched the figurine that had always stood on the inside window ledge. The Mother and Daughter Lladro that her daughter had bought her when she was married. Anger flooded Melissa's veins like a dam bursting.

'You bastard!' she screamed. 'You fucking bastard! Put that back!'

Startled, the man looked up her, and then bent to pick up the bundle at his feet. Frantic, Melissa grabbed the first thing that she could lay her hands on. A heavy glass bottle on the dressing table. As the burglar straightened up she hurled the bottle with all her might.

The man screamed, stumbled, dropped the bundle and put his hand to his head. Emboldened, Melissa grabbed another bottle, and another, raining them down on him, each accompanied by fierce invective. Leaving the bundle behind, the man staggered down the drive and onto the pavement where he broke into a hesitant jog that quickly became a sprint. To Melissa's dismay, his right hand still grasped the figurine.

With nothing left to attack, and the adrenalin leaching from her body, she sunk to her knees and began to weep.

The first to appear was Barry from next door in his dressing gown and slippers, clutching what looked suspiciously like a truncheon. He was joined by Geoff, from over the road, armed with a carving knife. Then Jack O'Riordan, the Neighbourhood Watch Co-ordinator from number seventeen, arrived holding a heavy duty torch.

'Melissa!' Barry shouted. 'It's alright, it's me, Barry. Come on down and open the door. Geoff and Jack are here. Let us in.'

'Where's Mike?' asked Geoff.

'Off on another of those jollies his firm calls training days,' Barry told him.

'Who's the key holder?' said Jack. 'She's obviously too frightened to come down. Anyway, she might be hurt. We can't just hang around out here till the police arrive.'

'I am,' said Barry. 'Shit, I didn't think to bring the key.'

'Well go and get it,' said Jack. There's no telling what state she's in. And take that bloody truncheon with you, and Geoff's knife. If the police see you two with those you're as likely to get arrested as the burglar.'

Melissa was in a terrible state. In shock, she shook from head to toe. While Geoff and Jack searched the house meticulously, she sat in the lounge wrapped in the duvet. Barry stayed with her while his wife brewed a pot of tea.

On the floor in front of them was the rug the thief had used to wrap up the items he had selected, all of which he'd left behind: an iPod and SoundDock, a Kindle, an iPad, the iPhone that had been on charge in the kitchen, the Christmas presents for each other that Melissa and Mike had placed beneath the tree, and a full bottle of whisky from the drinks cabinet. Melissa would happily have surrendered them all in exchange for the Mother and Daughter figurine he had taken.

By the time the police arrived, a half an hour later, she was beginning to recover.

'What took them so long?' Geoff whispered.

'They'll have been giving the bastard time to get clear so they wouldn't run the risk of coming up against a knife or a gun,' Barry replied, with the assurance of someone who knew about these things.

The constable who had taken her statement closed his pocket book with a sense of finality that seemed anything but promising, and stood up.

'Hell of a risk you took there,' he said to Melissa. 'Throwing that bottle at him willy nilly. If you'd killed him you realise you would have been facing a charge of manslaughter?'

'That's a bit harsh,' Geoff protested. 'She was only protecting her own home, and her property.'

'True,' he said. 'But not herself. He was leaving; he had his back to her. It was hardly self defence. No, she'd have been in real trouble and no mistake.' He saw the gleam in Barry's eyes. 'Don't blame us, he said holding up both hands like the innocent he was. 'We don't make up the rules. It's the CPS you want to complain to. Do us a favour if you did.'

When the police had gone they all agreed – though not in front of Melissa – that there seemed little likelihood that they would catch the thief or retrieve the precious Lladro. A forensic officer would call in the morning but if the burglar had been wearing gloves, and someone else's trainers, well – Geoff confided - they weren't going to go to the expense of full DNA analysis for the sake of a bit of china.

While the others were still there Melissa rang her husband. She'd been expecting him to shout at her for forgetting the alarm, and for not pressing the panic button at the side of the bed, but he must have sensed her distress. He told her not to worry, and that he would leave straight away. Barry stayed with her until Mike returned, an hour later.

It was 8 o'clock in the morning when the door bell went. Neither of them had been to bed.

'That'll be forensics,' said Mike getting up from the

kitchen table.

A man and a woman both dressed in plainclothes stood on the doorstep. He was stocky, the build of a rugby league forward. In his left hand he held a brown carrier bag. She was shorter, pretty, with auburn hair cut in a bob, and dark brown eyes that watched him intently. The man held up his identity card.

'Detective Inspector Holmes,' he said. 'This is DS Stuart. Can we come in?'

Mike ushered them in.

'Are you Forensics?'

'No,' Holmes replied curtly. 'Major Incidents. Is Mrs Wilsher in?'

'Through here,' he told them.

Melissa rose as they entered the room.

'This is Detective Inspector Holmes and Detective Sergeant Stuart,' said Mike. They would like a word with you.' He turned to the man. 'My wife has been up all night, and she's still a bit fragile. You'll go easy won't you?'

Holmes nodded curtly, reached into the bag and drew out a bloodstained hoodie top with Fat Face emblazoned across the front.

'Do you recognise this scent?' he asked.

Melissa didn't need to inspect it. It reeked of perfume.

'Yes,' she replied. 'That's one of mine. It's called Python.'

The two officers exchanged a meaningful glance.

'Does this mean you've caught him?' she asked.

Holmes placed the hoodie back in the bag. 'In a manner of speaking,' he said. 'The owner of this top, the one who you claim to have struck with a bottle, was taken to hospital in the early hours of this morning. He was dead on arrival.'

Melissa's hand went to her mouth; she gasped, and crumpled in a faint to the floor.

'Nice one Gordon,' muttered DS Stuart.

When Melissa came round Mike was kneeling anxiously beside her. There was a cushion beneath her head. The detectives hovered nearby.

'It's all right love,' Mike told her. 'It wasn't you that killed him.'

*****

It was ten to five in the morning, on Christmas Eve, when Wally Hubbard let himself into the cold dark house. He set the figurine down on the telephone table and tiptoed down the hallway to the kitchen. He opened the door, and switched on the light.

'Bloody Hell!' he exclaimed. 'You gave me a fright. What do you think you're doing woman?'

She studied him for a moment, standing there reeking of guilt, and some tart's cheap perfume. She'd suspected for months, hoping against hope, swallowing his lies. The lies that had begun shortly after their daughter had died in the hit-and-run. Him disappearing every evening leaving her to grieve alone. She leapt to her feet

'What have *you* been doing more like?' she screamed, launching herself at him, beating his chest with her fists.

He grasped her wrists and held them tightly.

'Sorting your Christmas present, you silly cow.'

'Liar! Liar! Liar!'

She struggled in vain to free herself, and began to kick out at his shins. He shifted his grip and pushed her away. She fell heavily against the faux marble work surface, and cried out in pain. He advanced, arms outstretched, to comfort her. She mistook his intention, reached out behind her, grabbed the first thing that she could find, and swung it violently towards him.

Wally stared uncomprehendingly at the handle of the six inch blade protruding from his chest. He staggered back. The corner of the kitchen table halted his progress. He slumped sideways and ended up sitting on the chair his wife had just vacated. A crimson stain spread slowly across the front of his hoodie. Blood bubbled from his mouth as tried to explain.

She was beyond listening, paralysed by the enormity of her actions, full of loathing for this man who had pushed her to it, amazed that she had put up with it for so long. She sat down opposite her husband, and watched as his life slipped away.

When it was over, she stood, went over to the sink, and splashed her face and the back of her neck with cold water. It was time to ring the police.

His head had slumped forward, and as she passed him she noticed a bloody clump of matted hair high up behind his ear. She had no idea how that had happened. Whatever, it hardly mattered now.

She sat on the bottom stair and began to dial.

'999: Hello. Which service do you require?'

She was about answer when she caught sight of the figurine on the telephone table. A mother cradling her daughter's head as she stared up at her. There was only one way it could have got there. Only one reason he would have brought it home on Christmas Eve. The phone slipped from her fingers.

She began to scream.

*****

DI Holmes closed his pocket book.

'That's what she told us,' he said. 'We've no reason to doubt her.'

There was an uncomfortable silence while Melissa tried to make sense of her emotions. Should she be feeling relief or sympathy, guilt even?

'My Lladro...this means you have it?' she said at last.

'We'll need it as evidence, but you'll get it back eventually' DS Stuart reassured her

'It looks like your perfume lived up to its reputation,' said Holmes.

Melissa stared at him. 'I'm sorry?'

'Python,' he said. 'To die for!'

The Author

Bill Rogers has written nine crime thriller novels to date – all of them based in and around the City of Manchester, and all in the top 10 bestsellers in the Kindle British Crime Fiction, Thriller, Police Procedural, and Detective categories. *Backwash* was a top 50 Bestseller across all fiction categories.

His first novel, *The Cleansing,* was short listed for the Long Barn Books Debut Novel Award. and received the *2011 ePublishing Consortium Writers' Award. A Trace of Blood,* reached the semi-final of the Amazon Breakthrough Novel Award.

The Books

The DCI Caton Crime Series

The Cleansing
The Head Case
The Tiger's Cave
A Fatal Intervention
Bluebell Hollow
A Trace of Blood
The Frozen Contract
Backwash
A Venetian Moon

And

The Cave
A novel for Teens, Young Adults, & Adults

Coming Soon
Angel Meadow
The Tenth DCI Tom Caton Novel

Available through Booksellers and online through Amazon, Waterstones and W H Smith in paperback.
also available as
Kindle eBooks

Lightning Source UK Ltd.
Milton Keynes UK
UKOW03f2248220514

232155UK00001B/2/P